The Angel Of The]

By

William Dean Howells

I.

"All that sort of personification," said Wanhope, "is far less remarkable than the depersonification which has now taken place so thoroughly that we no longer think in the old terms at all. It was natural that the primitive peoples should figure the passions, conditions, virtues, vices, forces, qualities, in some sort of corporal shape, with each a propensity or impulse of its own, but it does not seem to me so natural that the derivative peoples should cease to do so. It is rational that they should do so, and I don't know that any stronger proof of our intellectual advance could be alleged than the fact that the old personifications survive in the parlance while they are quite extinct in the consciousness. We still talk of death at times as if it were an embodied force of some kind, and of love in the same way; but I don't believe that any man of the commonest common-school education thinks of them so. If you try to do it yourself, you are rather ashamed of the puerility, and when a painter or a sculptor puts them in an objective shape, you follow him with impatience, almost with contempt."

"How about the poets?" asked Minver, less with the notion, perhaps, of refuting the psychologist than of bringing the literary member of our little group under the disgrace that had fallen upon him as an artist.

"The poets," said I, "are as extinct as the personifications."

"That's very handsome of you, Acton," said the artist. "But go on, Wanhope."

"Yes, get down to business," said Rulledge. Being of no employ whatever, and spending his whole life at the club in an extraordinary idleness, Rulledge was always using the most strenuous expressions, and requiring everybody to be practical. He leaned directly forward with the difficulty that a man of his girth has in such a movement, and vigorously broke off the ash of his cigar against the edge of his saucer. We had been dining together, and had been served with coffee in the Turkish room, as it was called from its cushions and hangings of Indian and Egyptian stuffs. "What is the instance you've got up your sleeve?" He smoked with great energy, and cast his eyes alertly about as if to make sure that there was no chance of Wanhope's physically escaping him, from the corner of the divan, where he sat pretty well hemmed in by the rest of us, spreading in an irregular circle before him.

"You unscientific people are always wanting an instance, as if an instance were convincing. An instance is only suggestive; a thousand instances, if you please, are convincing," said the psychologist. "But I don't know that I wish to be convincing. I would rather be enquiring. That is much more interesting, and, perhaps, profitable."

"All the same," Minver persisted, apparently in behalf of Rulledge, but with an after-grudge of his own, "you'll allow that you were thinking of something in particular when you began with that generalization about the lost art of personifying?"

"Oh, that is very curious," said the psychologist. "We talk of generalizing, but is there any such thing? Aren't we always striving from one concrete to another, and isn't what we call generalizing merely a process of finding our way?"

"I see what you mean," said the artist, expressing in that familiar formula the state of the man who hopes to know what the other man means.

"That's what I say," Rulledge put in. "You've got something up your sleeve. What is it?"

Wanhope struck the little bell on the table before him, but, without waiting for a response, he intercepted a waiter who was passing with a coffee-pot, and asked, "Oh, couldn't you give me some of that?"

The man filled his cup for him, and after Wanhope put in the sugar and lifted it to his lips, Rulledge said, with his impetuous business air, "It's easy to see what Wanhope does his high thinking on."

"Yes," the psychologist admitted, "coffee is an inspiration. But you can overdo an inspiration. It would be interesting to know whether there hasn't been a change in the quality of thought since the use of such stimulants came in-- whether it hasn't been subtilized--"

"Was that what you were going to say?" demanded Rulledge, relentlessly. "Come, we've got no time to throw away!"

Everybody laughed.

"_You_ haven't, anyway," said I.

"Well, none of his own," Minver admitted for the idler.

"I suppose you mean I have thrown it all away. Well, I don't want to throw away other peoples'. Go on, Wanhope."

II.

The psychologist set his cup down and resumed his cigar, which he had to pull at pretty strongly before it revived. "I should not be surprised," he began, "if a good deal of the fear of death had arisen, and perpetuated itself in the race, from the early personification of dissolution as an enemy of a certain dreadful aspect, armed and threatening. That conception wouldn't have been found in men's minds at first; it would have been the result of later crude meditation upon the fact. But it would have remained through all the imaginative ages, and the notion might have been intensified in the more delicate temperaments as time went on, and by the play of heredity it might come down to our own day in certain instances with a force scarcely impaired by the lapse of incalculable time."

"You said just now," said Rulledge, in rueful reproach, "that personification had gone out."

"Yes, it has. I did say that, and yet I suppose that though such a notion of death, say, no longer survives in the consciousness, it does survive in the unconsciousness, and that any vivid accident or illusory suggestion would have force to bring it to the surface."

"I wish I knew what you were driving at," said Rulledge.

"You remember Ormond, don't you?" asked Wanhope, turning suddenly to me.

"Perfectly," I said. "I--he isn't living, is he?"

"No; he died two years ago."

"I thought so," I said, with the relief that one feels in not having put a fellow-creature out of life, even conditionally.

"You knew Mrs. Ormond, too, I believe," the psychologist pursued.

I owned that I used to go to the Ormonds' house.

"Then you know what a type she was, I suppose," he turned to the others, "and as they're both dead it's no contravention of the club etiquette against talking of women, to speak of her. I can't very well give the instance--the sign--that Rulledge is seeking without speaking of her, unless I use a great deal of circumlocution." We all urged him to go on, and he went on. "I had the facts I'm going to give, from Mrs. Ormond. You know that the Ormonds left New York a couple of years ago?"

He happened to look at Minver as he spoke, and Minver answered: "No; I must confess that I didn't even know they had left the planet."

Wanhope ignored his irrelevant ignorance. "They went to live provisionally at a place up the Housatonic road, somewhere--perhaps Canaan; but it doesn't matter. Ormond had been suffering some time with an obscure affection of the heart--"

"Oh, come now!" said Rulledge. "You're not going to spring anything so pat as heart-disease on us?"

"Acton is all ears," said Minver, nodding toward me. "He hears the weird note afar."

The psychologist smiled. "I'm afraid you're not interested. I'm not much interested myself in these unrelated instances."

"Oh, no!" "Don't!" "Do go on!" the different entreaties came, and after a little time taken to recover his lost equanimity, Wanhope went on: "I don't know whether you knew that Ormond had rather a peculiar dread of death." We none of us could affirm that we did, and again Wanhope resumed: "I shouldn't say that he was a coward above other men I believe he was rather below the average in cowardice. But the thought of death weighed upon him. You find this much more commonly among the Russians, if we are to believe their novelists, than among Americans. He might have been a character out of one of Tourguénief's books, the idea of death was so constantly present with him. He once told me that the fear of it was a part of his earliest consciousness, before the time when he could have had any intellectual conception of it. It seemed to be something like the projection of an alien horror into his life--a prenatal influence--"

"Jove!" Rulledge broke in. "I don't see how the women stand it. To look forward nearly a whole year to death as the possible end of all they're hoping for and suffering for! Talk of men's courage after that! I wonder we're not _all_ marked.'

"I never heard of anything of the kind in Ormond's history," said Wanhope, tolerant of the incursion.

Minver took his cigar out to ask, the more impressively, perhaps, "What do you fellows make of the terror that a two months' babe starts in its sleep with before it can have any notion of what fear is on its own hook?"

"We don't make anything of it," the psychologist answered. "Perhaps the pathologists do."

"Oh, it's easy enough to say wind," Rulledge indignantly protested.

"Too easy, I agree with you," Wanhope consented. "We cannot tell what influences reach us from our environment, or what our environment really is, or how much or little we mean by the word. The sense of danger seems to be inborn, and possibly it is a survival of our race life when it was wholly animal and took care of itself through what we used to call the instincts. But, as I was saying, it was not danger that Ormond seemed to be afraid of, if it came short of death. He was almost abnormally indifferent to pain. I knew of his undergoing an operation that most people would take ether for, and not wincing, because it was not supposed to involve a fatal result.

"Perhaps he carried his own anodyne with him," said Minver, "like the Chinese."

"You mean a sort of self-anaesthesia?" Wanhope asked. "That is very interesting. How far such a principle, if there is one, can be carried in practice. The hypnotists--"

"I'm afraid I didn't mean anything so serious or scientific," said the painter.

"Then don't switch Wanhope off on a side track," Rulledge implored. "You know how hard it is to keep him on the main line. He's got a mind that splays all over the place if you give him the least chance. Now, Wanhope, come down to business."

Wanhope laughed amiably. "Why, there's so very little of the business. I'm not sure that it wasn't Mrs. Ormond's attitude toward the fact that interested me most. It was nothing short of devout. She was a convert. She believed he really saw--I suppose," he turned to me, "there's no harm in our recognizing now that they didn't always get on smoothly together?"

"Did they ever?" I asked.

"Oh, yes--oh, yes," said the psychologist, kindly. "They were very fond of each other, and often very peaceful."

"I never happened to be by," I said.

"Used to fight like cats and dogs," said Minver. "And they didn't seem to mind people. It was very swell, in a way, their indifference, and it did help to take away a fellow's embarrassment."

"That seemed to come mostly to an end that summer," said Wanhope, "if you could believe Mrs. Ormond."

"You probably couldn't," the painter put in.

"At any rate she seemed to worship his memory."

"Oh, yes; she hadn't him there to claw."

"Well, she was quite frank about it with me," the psychologist pursued. "She admitted that they had always quarreled a good deal. She seemed to think it was a token of their perfect unity. It was as if they were each quarreling with themselves, she said. I'm not sure that there wasn't something in the notion. There is no doubt but that they were tremendously in love with each other, and there is something curious in the bickerings of married people if they are in love. It's one way of having no concealments; it's perfect confidence of a kind--"

"Or unkind," Minver suggested.

"What has all that got to do with it!" Rulledge demanded.

"Nothing directly," Wanhope confessed, "and I'm not sure that it has much to do indirectly. Still, it has a certain atmospheric relation. It is very remarkable how thoughts connect themselves with one another. It's a sort of wireless telegraphy. They do not touch at all; there is apparently no manner of tie between them, but they communicate--"

"Oh, Lord!" Rulledge fumed.

Wanhope looked at him with a smiling concern, such as a physician might feel in the symptoms of a peculiar case. "I wonder," he said absently, "how much of our impatience with a fact delayed is a survival of the childhood of the race, and how far it is the effect of conditions in which possession is the ideal!"

Rulledge pushed back his chair, and walked away in dudgeon. "I'm a busy man myself. When you've got anything to say you can send for me."

Minver ran after him, as no doubt he meant some one should. "Oh, come back! He's just going to begin;" and when Rulledge, after some pouting, had been _pushed down into his chair again,_ Wanhope went on, with a glance of scientific pleasure at him.

III.

"The house they had taken was rather a lonely place, out of sight of neighbors, which they had got cheap because it was so isolated and inconvenient, I fancy. Of course Mrs. Ormond, with her exaggeration, represented it as a sort of solitude which nobody but tramps of the most dangerous description ever visited. As she said, she never went to sleep without expecting to wake up murdered in her bed."

"Like her," said Minver, with a glance at me full of relish for the touch of character which I would feel with him.

"She said," Wanhope went on, "that she was anxious from the first for the effect upon Ormond. In the stress of any danger, she gave me to understand, he always behaved very well, but out of its immediate presence he was full of all sorts of gloomy apprehensions, unless the surroundings were cheerful. She could not imagine how he came to take the place, but when she told him so--"

"I've no doubt she told him so pretty promptly," the painter grinned.

"--he explained that he had seen it on a brilliant day in spring, when all the trees were in bloom, and the bees humming in the blossoms, and the orioles singing, and the outlook from the lawn down over the river valley was at its best. He had fallen in love with the place, that was the truth, and he was so wildly in love with it all through that he could not feel the defect she did in it. He used to go gaily about the wide, harking old house at night, shutting it up, and singing or whistling while she sat quaking at the notion of their loneliness and their absolute helplessness--an invalid and a little woman--in case anything happened. She wanted him to get the man who did the odd jobs about the house, to sleep there, but he laughed at her, and they kept on with their usual town equipment of two serving-women. She could not account for his spirits, which were usually so low when they were alone--"

"And not fighting," Minver suggested to me.

"--and when she asked him what the matter was he could not account for them, either. But he said, one day, that the fear of death seemed to be lifted from his soul, and that made her shudder."

Rulledge fetched a long sigh, and Minver interpreted, "Beginning to feel that it's something like now."

"He said that for the first time within his memory he was rid of that nether consciousness of mortality which had haunted his whole life, and poisoned, more or less, all his pleasure in living. He had got a reprieve, or a respite, and he felt like a boy--another kind of boy from what he had ever been. He was full of all sorts of brilliant hopes and plans. He had visions of success in business beyond anything he had known, and talked of buying the place he had taken, and getting a summer colony of friends about them. He meant to cut the property up, and make the right kind of people inducements. His world seemed to have been emptied of all trouble as well as all mortal danger."

"Haven't you psychologists some message about a condition like that!" I asked.

"Perhaps it's only the pathologists again," said Minver.

"The alienists, rather more specifically," said Wanhope. "They recognize it as one of the beginnings of insanit--_folie des grandeurs_ as the French call the stage."

"Is it necessarily that?" Rulledge demanded, with a resentment which we felt so droll in him that we laughed.

"I don't know that it is," said Wanhope. "I don't know why we shouldn't sometimes, in the absence of proofs to the contrary, give such a fact the chance to evince a spiritual import. Of course it had no other import to poor Mrs.

Ormond, and of course I didn't dream of suggesting a scientific significance."

"I should think not!" Rulledge puffed.

Wanhope went on: "I don't think I should have dared to do so to a woman in her exaltation concerning it. I could see that however his state had affected her with dread or discomfort in the first place, it had since come to be her supreme hope and consolation. In view of what afterward happened, she regarded it as the effect of a mystical intimation from another world that was sacred, and could not he considered like an ordinary fact without sacrilege. There was something very pathetic in her absolute conviction that Ormond's happiness was an emanation from the source of all happiness, such as sometimes, where the consciousness persists, comes to a death-bed. That the dying are not afraid of dying is a fact of such common, such almost invariable observation--"

"You mean," I interposed, "when the vital forces are beaten so low that the natural dread of ceasing to be, has no play? It has less play, I've noticed, in age than in youth, but for the same reason that it has when people are weakened by sickness."

"Ah," said Wanhope, "that comparative indifference to death in the old, to whom it is so much nearer than it is to the young, is very suggestive. There may be something in what you say; they may not care so much because they have no longer the strength--the muscular strength--for caring. They are too tired to care as they used. There is a whole region of most important inquiry in that direction--"

"Did you mean to have him take that direction?" Rulledge asked, sulkily.

"He can take any direction for me," I said. "He is always delightful."

"Ah, thank you!" said Wanhope.

"But I confess," I went on, "that I was wondering whether the fact that the dying are indifferent to death could be established in the case of those who die in the flush of health and strength, like, for instance, people who are put to death."

Wanhope smiled. "I think it can--measurably. Most murderers make a good end, as the saying used to be, when they end on the scaffold, though they are not supported by religious fervor of any kind, or the exaltation of a high ideal. They go meekly and even cheerfully to their death, without rebellion or even objection. It is most exceptional that they make a fight for their lives, as that woman did a few years ago at Dannemora, and disgusted all refined people with capital punishment."

"I wish they would make a fight always," said Rulledge, with unexpected feeling. "It would do more than anything to put an end to that barbarity."

"It would be very interesting, as Wanhope says," Minver remarked. "But aren't we getting rather far away? From the Ormonds, I mean."

"We are, rather," said Wanhope. "Though I agree that it would be interesting. I should rather like to have it tried. You know Frederick Douglass acted upon some such principle when his master attempted to whip him. He fought, and he had a theory that if the slave had always fought there would soon have been an end of whipping, and so an end of slavery. But probably it will be a good while before criminals are--"

"Educated up to the idea," Minver proposed.

"Yes," Wanhope absently acquiesced. "There seems to be a resignation intimated to the parting soul, whether in sickness or in health, by the mere proximity of death. In Ormond's case there seems to have been something more positive. His wife says that in the beginning of those days he used to come to her and wonder what could be the matter with him. He had a joy he could not account for by anything in their lives, and it made her tremble."

"Probably it didn't. I don't think there was anything that could make Mrs. Ormond tremble, unless it was the chance that Ormond would get the last word," said Minver.

No one minded him, and Wanhope continued: "Of course she thought he must be going to have a fit of sickness, as the people say in the country, or used to say. Those expressions often survive in the common parlance long after the peculiar mental and moral conditions in which they originated have passed away. They must once have been more accurate than they are now. When one said 'fit of sickness' one must have meant something specific; it would be interesting to know what. Women use those expressions longer than men; they seem to be inveterate in their nerves; and women apparently do their thinking in their nerves rather than their brains."

IV.

Wanhope had that distant look in his eyes which warned his familiars of a possible excursion, and I said, in the hope of keeping him from it, "Then isn't there a turn of phrase somewhat analogous to that in a personification?"

"Ah, yes--a personification," he repeated with a freshness of interest, which he presently accounted for. "The place they had taken was very completely furnished. They got it fully equipped, even to linen and silver; but what was more important to poor Ormond was the library, very rich in the English classics, which appeared to go with the house. The owner was a girl who married and lived abroad, and these were her father's books. Mrs. Ormond said that her husband had the greatest pleasure in them: their print, which was good and black, and their paper, which was thin and yellowish, and their binding, which was tree calf in the poets, he specially liked. They were English editions as well as English classics, and she said he caressed the books, as he read them, with that touch which the book-lover has; he put his face into them, and inhaled their odor as if it were the bouquet of wine; he wanted her to like it, too."

"Then she hated it," Minver said, unrelentingly.

"Perhaps not, if there was nobody else there," I urged.

For once Wanhope was not to be tempted off on another scent. "There was a good deal of old-fashioned fiction of the suspiratory and exclamatory sort, like Mackenzie's, and Sterne's and his followers, full of feeling, as people understood feeling a hundred years ago. But what Ormond rejoiced in most were the poets, good and bad, like Gray and Collins and Young, and their contemporaries, who personified nearly everything from Contemplation to Indigestion, through the whole range of the Vices, Virtues, Passions, Propensities, Attributes, and Qualities, and gave them each a dignified capital letter to wear. She said he used to come roaring to her with the passages in which these personifications flourished, and read them off with mock admiration, and then shriek and sputter with laughter. You know the way he had when a thing pleased him, especially a thing that had some relish of the quaint or rococo. As nearly as she would admit, in view of his loss, he bored her with these things. He was always hunting down some new personification, and when he had got it, adding it to the list he kept. She said he had thousands of them, but I suppose he had not so many. He had enough, though, to keep him amused, and she said he talked of writing something for the magazines about them, but probably he never would have done it. He never wrote anything, did he?" Wanhope asked of me.

"Oh, no. He was far too literary for _that_," I answered. "He had a reputation to lose."

"Pretty good," said Minver, "even if Ormond _is_ dead."

Wanhope ignored us both. "After awhile, his wife said, she began to notice a certain change in his attitude toward the personifications. She noticed this, always expecting that fit of sickness for him; but she was not so much troubled by his returning seriousness. Oh, I ought to tell you that when she first began to be anxious for him she privately wrote home to their family doctor, telling him how strangely happy Ormond was, and asking him if he could advise anything. He wrote back that if Ormond was so very happy they had better not do anything to cure him; that the disease was not infectious, and was seldom fatal."

"What an ass!" said Rulledge.

"Yes, I think he was, in this instance. But probably he had been consulted a good deal by Mrs. Ormond," said Wanhope. "The change that began to set her mind at rest about Ormond was his taking the personifications more seriously. Why, he began to ask, but always with a certain measure of joke in it, why shouldn't there be something _in_ the personifications? Why shouldn't Morn and Eve come corporeally walking up their lawn, with little or no clothes on, or Despair be sitting in their woods with her hair over her face, or Famine coming gauntly up to their back door for a hand-out? Why shouldn't they any day see pop-eyed Rapture passing on the trolley, or Meditation letting the car she intended to take go by without stepping lively enough to get on board? He pretended that we could have the personifications back again, if we were not so conventional in our conceptions of them. He wanted to know what reason there was for representing Life as a very radiant and bounding party, when Life usually neither shone nor bounded; and why Death should be figured as an enemy with a dart, when it was so often the only friend a man had left, and had the habit of binding up wounds rather than inflicting them. The personifications were all right, he said, but the poets and painters did not know how they really looked. By the way," Wanhope broke off, "did you happen to see Hauptmann's 'Hånnele' when it was here?"

None of us had, and we waited rather restively for the passing of the musing fit which he fell into. After a while he resumed at a point whose relation to the matter in hand we could trace:

"It was extremely interesting for all reasons, by its absolute fearlessness and freshness in regions where there has been nothing but timid convention for a long time; but what I was thinking of was the personification of Death as it appears there. The poor little dying pauper, lying in her dream at the almshouse, sees the figure of Death. It is not the skeleton with the dart, or the phantom with the shrouded face, but a tall, beautiful young man,--as beautiful as they could get into the cast, at any rate,--clothed in simple black, and standing with his back against the mantlepiece, with his hands resting on the hilt of a long, two-handed sword. He is so quiet that you do not see him until some time after the child has seen him. When she begins to question him whether she may not somehow get to heaven without dying, he answers with a sort of sorrowful tenderness, a very sweet and noble compassion, but unsparingly as to his mission. It is a singular moment of pure poetry that makes the heart ache, but does not crush or terrify the spirit."

"And what has it got to do with Ormond?" asked Rulledge, but with less impatience than usual.

"Why, nothing, I'm afraid, that I can make out very clearly. And yet there is an obscure connection with Ormond, or his vision, if it was a vision. Mrs. Ormond could not be very definite about what he saw, perhaps because even at the last moment he was not definite himself. What she was clear about, was the fact that his mood, though it became more serious, by no means became sadder. It became a sort of solemn joy instead of the light gaiety it had begun by being. She was no sort of scientific observer, and yet the keenness of her affection made her as closely observant of Ormond as if she had been studying him psychologically. Sometimes the light in his room would wake her at night, and she would go to him, and find him lying with a book faced down on his breast, as if he had been reading, and his fingers interlaced under his head, and a kind of radiant peace in his face. The poor thing said that when she would ask him what the matter was, he would say, 'Nothing; just happiness,' and when she would ask him if he did not think he ought to do something, he would laugh, and say perhaps it would go off of itself. But it did not go off; the unnatural buoyancy continued after he became perfectly tranquil. 'I don't know,' he would say. 'I seem to have got to the end of my troubles. I haven't a care in the world, Jenny. I don't believe you could get a rise out of me if you said the nastiest thing you could think of. It sounds like nonsense, of course, but it seems to me that I have found out the reason of things, though I don't know what it is. Maybe I've only found out that there _is_ a reason of things. That would be enough, wouldn't it?'"

V.

At this point Wanhope hesitated with a kind of diffidence that was rather charming in him. "I don't see," he said, "just how I can keep the facts from this on out of the line of facts which we are not in the habit of respecting very much, or that we relegate to the company of things that are not facts at all. I suppose that in stating them I shall somehow make myself responsible for them, but that is just what I don't want to do. I don't want to do anything more than give them as they were given to me."

"You won't be able to give them half as fully," said Minver, "if Mrs. Ormond gave them to you."

"No," Wanhope said gravely, "and that's the pity of it; for they ought to be given as fully as possible."

"Go ahead," Rulledge commanded, "and do the best you can."

"I'm not sure," the psychologist thoughtfully said, "that I am quite satisfied to call Ormond's experiences hallucinations. There ought to be some other word that doesn't accuse his sanity in that degree. For he apparently didn't show any other signs of an unsound mind."

"None that Mrs. Ormond would call so," Minver suggested.

"Well, in his case, I don't think she was such a bad judge," Wanhope returned. "She was a tolerably unbalanced person herself, but she wasn't altogether disqualified for observing him, as I've said before. They had a pretty hot summer, as the summer is apt to be in the Housatonic valley, but when it got along into September the weather was divine, and they spent nearly the whole time out of doors, driving over the hills. They got an old horse from a native, and they hunted out a rickety buggy from the carriage-house, and they went wherever the road led. They went mostly at a walk, and that suited the horse exactly, as well as Mrs. Ormond, who had no faith in Ormond's driving, and wanted to go at a pace that would give her a chance to jump out safely if anything happened. They put their hats in the front of the buggy, and went about in their bare heads. The country people got used to them, and were not scandalized by their appearance, though they were both getting a little gray, and must have looked as if they were old enough to know better.

"They were not really old, as age goes nowadays: he was not more than forty-two or -three, and she was still in the late thirties. In fact, they were

Nel mezzo del cammin di nostra vita--

in that hour when life, and the conceit of life, is strongest, and when it feels as if it might go on forever. Women are not very articulate about such things, and it was probably Ormond who put their feeling into words, though she recognized at once that it was her feeling, and shrank from it as if it were something wicked, that they would be punished for; so that one day, when he said suddenly, 'Jenny, I don't feel as if I could ever die,' she scolded him for it. Poor women!" said Wanhope, musingly, "they are not always cross when they scold. It is often the expression of their anxieties, their forebodings, their sextimidities. They are always in double the danger that men are, and their nerves double that danger again. Who was that famous _salonnière_--Mme. Geoffrin, was it?--that Marmontel says always scolded her friends when they were in trouble, and came and scolded him when he was put into the Bastille? I suppose Mrs. Ormond was never so tender of Ormond as she was when she took it out of him for suggesting what she wildly felt herself, and felt she should pay for feeling."

Wanhope had the effect of appealing to Minver, but the painter would not relent. "I don't know. I've seen her--or heard her--in very devoted moments."

"At any rate," Wanhope resumed, "she says she scolded him, and it did not do the least good. She could not scold him out of that feeling, which was all mixed up in her retrospect with the sense of the weather and the season, the leaves just beginning to show the autumn, the wild asters coming to crowd the goldenrod, the crickets shrill in the grass, and the birds silent in the trees, the smell of the rowan in the meadows, and the odor of the old logs and fresh chips in the woods. She was not a woman to notice such things much, but he talked of them all and made her notice them. His nature took hold upon what we call nature, and clung fondly to the lowly and familiar aspects of it. Once she said to him, trembling for him, 'I should think you would be afraid to take such a pleasure in those things,' and when he asked her why, she couldn't or wouldn't tell him; but he understood, and he said: 'I've never realized before that I was so much a part of them. Either I am going to have them forever, or they are going to have me. We shall not part, for we are all members of the same body. If it is the body of death, we are members of that. If it is the body of life, we are members of that. Either I have never lived, or else I am never going to die.' She said: 'Of course you are never going to die; a spirit can't die.' But he told her he didn't mean that. He was just as radiantly happy when they would get home from one of their drives, and sit down to their supper, which they had country-fashion instead of dinner, and then when they would turn into their big, lamplit parlor, and sit down for a long evening with his books. Sometimes he read to her as she sewed, but he read mostly to himself, and he said he hadn't had such a bath of poetry since he was a boy. Sometimes in the splendid nights, which were so clear that you could catch the silver glint of the gossamers in the thin air, he would go out and walk up and down the long veranda. Once, when he coaxed her out with him, he took her under the arm and walked her up and down, and he said: 'Isn't it like a ship? The earth is like a ship, and we're sailing, sailing! Oh, I wonder where!' Then he stopped with a sob, and she was startled, and asked him what the matter was, but he couldn't tell her. She was more frightened than ever at what seemed a break in his happiness. She was troubled about his reading the Bible so much, especially the Old Testament; but he told her he had never known before what majestic literature it was. There were some turns or phrases in it that peculiarly took his fancy and seemed to feed it with inexhaustible suggestion. 'The Angel of the Lord' was one of these. The idea of a divine messenger, embodied and commissioned to intimate the creative will to the creature: it was sublime, it was ineffable. He wondered that men had ever come to think in any other terms of the living law that we were under, and that could much less conceivably operate like an insensate mechanism than it could reveal itself as a constant purpose. He said he believed that in every great moral crisis, in every ordeal of conscience, a man was aware of standing in the presence of something sent to try him and test him, and that this something was the Angel of the Lord.

"He went off that night, saying to himself, 'The Angel of the Lord, the Angel of the Lord!' and when she lay a long time awake, waiting for him to go to sleep, she heard him saying it again in his room. She thought he might be dreaming, but when she went to him, he had his lamp lighted, and was lying with that rapt smile on his face which she was so afraid of. She told him she was afraid and she wished he would not say such things; and that made him laugh, and he put his arms round her, and laughed and laughed, and said it was only a kind of swearing, and she must cheer up. He let her give him some trional to make him sleep, and then she went off to her bed again. But when they both woke late, she heard him, as he dressed, repeating fragments of verse, quoting quite without order, as the poem drifted through his memory. He told her at breakfast that it was a poem which Longfellow had written to Lowell upon the occasion of his wife's death, and he wanted to get it and read it to her. She said she did not see how he could let his mind run on such gloomy things. But he protested he was not the least gloomy, and that he supposed his recollection of the poem was a continuation of his thinking about the Angel of the Lord.

"While they were at table a tramp came up the drive under the window, and looked in at them hungrily. He was a very offensive tramp, and quite took Mrs. Ormond's appetite away: but Ormond would not send him round to the kitchen, as she wanted; he insisted upon taking him a plate and a cup of coffee out on the veranda himself. When she expostulated with him, he answered fantastically that the fellow might be an angel of the Lord, and he asked her if she remembered Parnell's poem of 'The Hermit.' Of course she didn't, but he needn't get it, for she didn't want to hear it, and if he kept making her so nervous, she should be sick herself. He insisted upon telling her what the poem was, and how the angel in it had made himself abhorrent to the hermit by throttling the babe of the good man who had housed and fed them, and committing other atrocities, till the hermit couldn't stand it any longer, and the angel explained that he had done it all to prevent the greater harm that would have come if he had not killed and stolen in season. Ormond laughed at her disgust, and said he was curious to see what a tramp would do that was treated with real hospitality. He thought they had made a mistake in not asking this tramp in to breakfast with them; then they might have stood a chance of being murdered in their beds to save them from mischief."

VI.

"Mrs. Ormond really lost her patience with him, and felt better than she had for a long time by scolding him in good earnest. She told him he was talking very blasphemously, and when he urged that his morality was directly in line with Parnell's, and Parnell was an archbishop, she was so vexed that she would not go to drive with him that morning, though he apologized and humbled himself in every way. He pleaded that it was such a beautiful day, it must be the last they were going to have; it was getting near the equinox, and this must be a weather-breeder. She let him go off alone, for he would not lose the drive, and she watched him out of sight from her upper window with a heavy heart. As soon as he was fairly gone, she wanted to go after him, and she was wild all the forenoon. She could not stay indoors, but kept walking up and down the piazza and looking for him, and at times she went a bit up the road he had taken, to meet him. She had got to thinking of the tramp, though the man had gone directly off down another road after he had his breakfast. At last she heard the old creaking, rattling buggy, and as soon as she saw Ormond's bare head, and knew he was all right, she ran up to her room and shut herself in. But she couldn't hold out against him when he came to her door with an armful of wild flowers that he had gathered for her, and boughs from some young maples that he had found all red in a swamp. She showed herself so interested that he asked her to come with him after their midday dinner and see them, and she said perhaps she would, if he would promise not to keep talking about the things that made her so miserable. He asked her, 'What things?' and she answered that he knew well enough, and he laughed and promised.

"She didn't believe he would keep his word, but he did at first, and he tried not to tease her in any way. He tried to please her in the whims and fancies she had about going this way or that, and when she decided not to look up his young maples with him, because the first autumn leaves made her melancholy, he submitted. He put his arm across her shoulder as they drove through the woods, and pulled her to him, and called her 'poor old thing,' and accused her of being morbid. He wanted her to tell him all there was in her mind, but she could not; she could only cry on his arm. He asked her if it was something about him that troubled her, and she could only say that she hated to see people so cheerful without reason. That made him laugh, and they were very gay after she had got her cry out; but he grew serious again. Then her temper rose, and she asked, 'Well, what is it?' and he said at first, 'Oh, nothing,' as people do when there is really something, and presently he confessed that he was thinking about what she had said of his being cheerful without reason. Then, as she said, he talked so beautifully that she had to keep her patience with him, though he was not keeping his word to her. His talk, as far as she was able to report it, didn't amount to much more than this: that in a world where death was, people never could be cheerful with reason unless death was something altogether different from what people imagined. After people came to their intellectual consciousness, death was never wholly out of it, and if they could be joyful with that black drop at the bottom of every cup, it was proof positive that death was not what it seemed. Otherwise there was no logic in the scheme of being, but it was a cruel fraud by the Creator upon the creature; a poor practical joke, with the laugh all on one side. He had got rid of his fear of it in that light, which seemed to have come to him before the fear left him, and he wanted her to see it in the same light, and if he died before her--But there she stopped him and protested that it would kill her if she did not die first, with no apparent sense, even when she told me, of her fatuity, which must have amused poor Ormond. He said what he wanted to ask was that she would believe he had not been the least afraid to die, and he wished her to remember this always, because she knew how he always used to be afraid of dying. Then he really began to talk of other things, and he led the way back to the times of their courtship and their early married days, and their first journeys together, and all their young-people friends, and the simple-hearted pleasure they used to take in society, in teas and dinners, and going to the theater. He did not like to think how that pleasure had dropped out of their life, and he did not know why they had let it, and he was going to have it again when they went to town.

"They had thought of staying a long time in the country, perhaps till after Thanksgiving, for they had become attached to their place; but now they suddenly agreed to go back to New York at once. She told me that as soon as they agreed she felt a tremendous longing to be gone that instant, as if she must go to escape from something, some calamity, and she felt, looking back, that there was a prophetic quality in her eagerness."

"Oh, she was always so," said Minver. "When a thing was to be done, she wanted it done like lightning, no matter what the thing was."

"Well, very likely," Wanhope consented. "I never make much account of those retroactive forebodings. At any rate, she says she wanted him to turn about and drive home so that they could begin packing, and when he demurred, and began to tease, as she called it, she felt as if she should scream, till he turned the old horse and took the back track. She was _wild_ to get home, and kept hurrying him, and wanting him to whip the horse; but the old horse merely wagged his tail, and declined to go faster than a walk, and this was the only thing that enabled her to forgive herself afterward."

"Why, what had she done?" Rulledge asked. "She would have been responsible for what happened, according to her notion, if she had had her way with the horse; she would have felt that she had driven Ormond to his doom."

"Of course!" said Minver. "She always found a hole to creep out of. Why couldn't she go back a little further, and hold herself responsible through having made him turn round?"

"Poor woman!" said Rulledge, with a tenderness that made Minver smile. "What was it that did happen?"

Wanhope examined his cup for some dregs of coffee, and then put it down with an air of resignation. I offered to touch the bell, but, "No, don't," he said. "I'm better without it." And he went on: "There was a lonely piece of woods that they had to drive through before they struck the avenue leading to their house, which was on a cheerful upland overlooking the river, and when they had got about half-way through this woods, the tramp whom Ormond had fed in the morning, slipped out of a thicket on the hillside above them, and crossed the road in front of them, and slipped out of sight among the trees on the slope below. Ormond stopped the horse, and turned to his wife with a strange kind of whisper. 'Did you see it?' he asked, and she answered yes, and bade him drive on. He did so, slowly looking back round the side of the buggy till a turn of the road hid the place where the tramp had crossed their track. She could not speak, she says, till they came in sight of their house. Then her heart gave a great bound, and she broke out on him, blaming him for having encouraged the tramp to lurk about, as he must have done, all day, by his foolish sentimentality in taking his breakfast out to him.

'He saw that you were a delicate person, and now to-night he will be coming round, and--' She says Ormond kept looking at her, while she talked, as if he did not know what she was saying, and all at once she glanced down at their feet, and discovered that her hat was gone.

"That, she owned, made her frantic, and she blazed out at him again, and accused him of having lost her hat by stopping to look at that worthless fellow, and then starting up the horse so suddenly that it had rolled out. He usually gave her as good as she sent when she let herself go in that way, and she told me she would have been glad if he had done it now, but he only looked at her in a kind of daze, and when he understood, at last, he bade her get out and go into the house--they were almost at the door,--and he would go back and find her hat himself. 'Indeed, you'll do nothing of the kind,' she said she told him. 'I shall go back with you, or you'll be hunting up that precious vagabond and bringing him home to supper.' Ormond said, 'All right,' with a kind of dreamy passivity, and he turned the old horse again, and they drove slowly back, looking for the hat in the road, right and left. She had not noticed before that it was getting late, and perhaps it was not so late as it seemed when they got into that lonely piece of woods again, and the veils of shadow began to drop round them, as if they were something falling from the trees, she said. They found the hat easily enough at the point where it must have rolled out of the buggy, and he got down and picked it up. She kept scolding him, but he did not seem to hear her. He stood dangling the hat by its ribbons from his right hand, while he rested his left on the dashboard, and looking--looking down into the wooded slope where the tramp had disappeared. A cold chill went over her, and she stopped her scolding. 'Oh, Jim,' she said, 'do you see something? What do you see?' He flung the hat from him, and ran plunging down the hillside-- she covered up her face when she told me, and said she should always see him running--till the dusk among the trees hid him. She ran after him, and she heard him calling, calling joyfully, 'Yes, I'm coming!' and she thought he was calling back to her, but the rush of his feet kept getting farther, and then he seemed to stop with a sound like falling. He couldn't have been much ahead of her, for it was only a moment till she stood on the edge of a boulder in the woods, looking over, and there at the bottom Ormond was lying with his face turned under him, as she expressed it; and the tramp, with a heavy stick in his hand, was standing by him, stooping over him, and staring at him. She began to scream, and it seemed to her that she flew down from the brink of the rock, and caught the tramp and clung to him, while she kept screaming 'Murder!' The man didn't try to get away; he only said, over and over, 'I didn't touch him, lady; I didn't touch him.' It all happened simultaneously, like events in a dream, and while there was nobody there but herself and the tramp, and Ormond lying between them, there were some people that must have heard her from the road and come down to her. They were neighbor-folk that knew her and Ormond, and they naturally laid hold of the tramp; but he didn't try to escape. He helped them gather poor Ormond up, and he went back to the house with them, and staid while one of them ran for the doctor. The doctor could only tell them that Ormond was dead, and that his neck must have been broken by his fall over the rock. One of the neighbors went to look at the place the next morning, and found one of the roots of a young tree growing on the rock, torn out, as if Ormond had caught his foot in it; and that had probably made his fall a headlong dive. The tramp knew nothing but that he heard shouting and running, and got up from the foot of the rock, where he was going to pass the night, when something came flying through the air, and struck at his feet. Then it scarcely stirred, and the next thing, he said, the lady was _onto_ him, screeching and tearing. He piteously protested his innocence, which was apparent enough, at the inquest, and before, for that matter. He said Ormond was about the only man that ever treated him white, and Mrs. Ormond was remorseful for having let him get away before she could tell him that she didn't blame him, and ask him to forgive her."

VII.

Wanhope desisted with a provisional air, and Rulledge went and got Himself a sandwich from the lunch-table.

"Well, upon my word!" said Minver. "I thought you had dined, Rulledge."

Rulledge came back munching, and said to Wanhope, as he settled himself in his chair again: "Well, go on."

"Why, that's all."

The psychologist was silent, with Rulledge staring indignantly at him.

"I suppose Mrs. Ormond had her theory?" I ventured.

"Oh, yes--such as it was," said Wanhope. "It was her belief--her religion--that Ormond had seen Death, in person or personified, or the angel of it; and that the sight was something beautiful, and not terrible. She thought that she should see Death, too in the same way, as a messenger. I don't know that it was such a bad theory," he added impartially.

"Not," said Minver, "if you suppose that Ormond was off his nut. But, in regard to the whole matter, there is always a question of how much truth there was in what she said about it."

"Of course," the psychologist admitted, "that is a question which must be considered. The question of testimony in such matters is the difficult thing. You might often believe in supernatural occurrences if it were not for the witnesses. It is very interesting," he pursued, with his scientific smile, "to note how corrupting anything supernatural or mystical is. Such things seem mostly to happen either in the privity of people who are born liars, or else they deprave the spectator so, through his spiritual vanity or his love of the marvelous, that you can't believe a word he says.

"They are as bad as horses on human morals," said Minver. "Not that I think it ever needed the coming of a ghost to invalidate any statement of Mrs. Ormond's." Rulledge rose and went away growling something, partially audible, to the disadvantage of Minver's wit, and the painter laughed after him: "He really believes it."

Wanhope's mind seemed to be shifted from Mrs. Ormond to her convert, whom he followed with his tolerant eyes. "Nothing in all this sort of inquiry is so impossible to predicate as the effect of any given instance upon a given mind. It would be very interesting--"

"Excuse me!" said Minver. "There's Whitley. I must speak to him."

He went away, leaving me alone with the psychologist.

"And what is your own conclusion in this instance?" I asked.

"Why, I haven't formulated it yet."

THOUGH ONE ROSE FROM THE DEAD.

I.

You are very welcome to the Alderling incident, my dear Acton, if you think you can do anything with it, and I will give it as circumstantially as possible. The thing has its limitations, I should think, for the fictionist, chiefly in a sort of roundedness which leaves little play to the imagination. It seems to me that it would be more to your purpose if it were less _pat_, in its catastrophe, but you are a better judge of all that than I am, and I will put the facts in your hands, and keep my own hands off, so far as any plastic use of the material is concerned.

The first I knew of the peculiar Alderling situation was shortly after William James's "Will to Believe" came out. I had been telling the Alderlings about it, for they had not seen it, and I noticed that from time to time they looked significantly at each other. When I had got through he gave a little laugh, and she said, "Oh, you may laugh!" and then I made bold to ask, "What is it?"

"Marion can tell you," he said. He motioned towards the coffee-pot and asked,

"More?" I shook my head, and he said, "Come out and let us see what the maritime interests have been doing for us. Pipe or cigar?" I chose cigarettes, and he brought the box off the table, stopping on his way to the veranda, and taking his pipe and tobacco-pouch from the hall mantel.

Mrs. Alderling had got to the veranda before us, and done things to the chairs and cushions, and was leaning against one of the slender fluted pine columns like some rich, blond caryatid just off duty, with the blue of her dress and the red of her hair showing deliciously against the background of white house-wall. He and she were an astonishing and satisfying contrast; in the midst of your amazement you felt the divine propriety of a woman like her wanting just such a wiry, smoky-complexioned, black-browed, black-bearded, bald-headed little man as he was. Before he sat down where she was going to put him, he stood stoopingly, and frowned at the waters of the cove lifting from the foot of the lawn that sloped to it before the house. "Three lumbermen, two goodish-sized yachts, a dozen sloop-rigged boats: not so bad. About the usual number that come loafing in to spend the night. You ought to see them when it threatens to breeze up. Then they're here in flocks. Go on, Marion."

He gave a soft groan of comfort as he settled in his chair and began pulling at his short black pipe, and she let her eyes dwell on him in a rapture that curiously interested me. People in love are rarely interesting--that is, flesh-and-blood people. Of course I know that lovers are the life of fiction, and that a story of any kind can scarcely hold the reader without them. The love-interest, as they call it, is also supposed to be essential to the drama, and friends of mine who have tried to foist their plays upon managers have been overthrown by the objection that the love-interest is not strong enough in what they have done. Yet lovers in real life are, so far as I have observed them, bores. They are confessed to be disgusting before or after marriage when they let their fondness appear, but even when they try to hide it, they are tiresome. Character goes down before passion in them; nature is reduced to propensity. Then, how is it that the novelist manages to keep these, and to give us nature and character while seeming to offer nothing but propensity and passion? Perhaps he does not give them. Perhaps what he does is to hypnotize us so that we each of us identify ourselves with the lovers, and add our own natures and characters to the single principle that animates them. The reason we like, that we endure, to read about them, may be that they are ourselves rendered objective in an instant of intense vitality, without the least trouble or risk to us. But if we have them there before us in the tiresome reality, they exclude us from their pleasure in each other and stop up the perspective of our happiness with their hulking personalities, bare of all the iridescence of potentiality, which we could have cast about them. Something of this iridescence may cling to unmarried lovers, in spite of themselves, but wedded bliss is a sheer offence.

I do not know why it was not an offence in the case of the Alderlings, unless it was because they both, in their different ways, saw the joke of the thing. At any rate, I found that in their charm for each other they had somehow not ceased to be amusing for me, and I waited confidently for the answer she would make to his whimsically abrupt bidding. But she did not answer very promptly, even when he had added, "Wanhope, here, is scenting something psychological in the reason of my laughing at you, instead of accepting the plain inference in the case."

"What is the plain inference?" I asked, partly to fill up Mrs. Alderling's continued silence.

"When a man laughs at a woman for no apparent reason it is because he is amused at her being afraid of him when he is so much more afraid of her, or puzzled by him when she is such an incomparable riddle herself, or caring for him when he knows he is not worth his salt."

"You don't expect to put me off with that sort of thing," I said.

"Well, then, go on Marion," Alderling repeated.

II.

Mrs. Alderling stood looking at him, not me, with a smile hovering about the corners of her mouth, which, when it decided not to alight anywhere, scarcely left her aspect graver for its flitting. She said at last, in her slow, deep-throated voice, "I guess I will let you tell him."

"Oh, I'll tell him fast enough," said Alderling, nursing his knee, and bringing it well up toward his chin, between his clasped hands. "Marion has always had the notion that I should live again if I believed I should, and that as I don't believe I shall, I am not going to. The joke of it is," and he began to splutter laughter round the stem of his pipe, "she's as much of an agnostic as I am. She doesn't believe she is going to live again, either."

Mrs. Alderling said, "I don't care for it in my case." That struck me as rather touching, but I had no right to enter uninvited into the intimacy of her meaning, and I said, looking as little at her as I need, "Aren't you both rather belated?"

"You mean that protoplasm has gone out?" he chuckled.

"Not exactly," I answered. "But you know that a great many things are allowed now that were once forbidden to the True Disbeliever."

"You mean that we may trust in the promises, as they used to be called, and still keep the Unfaith?"

"Something like that."

Alderling took his pipe out, apparently to give his whole face to the pleasure of teasing his wife.

"That'll be a great comfort to Marion," he said, and he threw back his head and laughed.

She smiled faintly, vaguely, tolerantly, as if she enjoyed his pleasure in teasing her.

"Where have you been," I asked, "that you don't know the changed attitude in these matters?"

"Well, here for the last three years. We tried it the first winter after we came, and found it was not so bad, and we simply stayed on. But I haven't really looked into the question since I gave the conundrum up twenty years ago, on what was then the best authority. Marion doesn't complain. She knew what I was when she married me. She was another. We were neither of us very bigoted disbelievers. We should not have burned anybody at the stake for saying that we had souls."

Alderling put back his pipe and cackled round it, taking his knee between his hands again.

"You know," she explained, more in my direction than to me, "that I had none to begin with. But Alderling had. His people believed in the future life."

"That's what they said," Alderling crowed. "And Marion has always thought that if she had believed that way, she could have kept me up to it; and so when I died I should have lived again. It is perfectly logical, though it isn't capable of a practical demonstration. If Marion had come of a believing family, she could have brought me back into the fold. Her great mistake was in being brought up by an uncle who denied that he was living here, even. The poor girl could not do a thing when it came to the life hereafter."

The smile now came hovering back, and alighted at a corner of Mrs. Alderling's mouth, making it look, oddly enough, rather rueful. "It didn't matter about me. I thought it a pity that Alderling's talent should stop here."

"Did you ever know anything like that?" he cried. "Perfectly willing to thrust me out into a cold other-world, and leave me to struggle on without her, when I had got used to her looking after me. Now I'm not so selfish as that. I shouldn't want to have Marion living on through all eternity if I wasn't with her. It would be too lonely for her."

He looked up at her, with his dancing eyes, and she put her hand down over his shoulder into the hand that he lifted to meet it, in a way that would have made me sick in some people. But in her the action was so casual, so absent, that it did not affect me disagreeably.

"Do you mean that you haven't been away since you came here three years ago?" I asked.

"We ran up to the theatre once in Boston last winter, but it bored us to the limit." Alderling poked his knife-blade into the bowl of his pipe as he spoke, having freed his hand for the purpose, while Mrs. Alderling leaned back against the slim column again. He said gravely: "It was a great thing for Marion, though. In view of the railroad accident that didn't happen, she convinced herself that her sole ambition was that we should die together. Then, whether we found ourselves alive or not, we should be company for each other. She's got it arranged with the thunderstorms, so that one bolt will do for us both, and she never lets me go out on the water alone, for fear I shall watch my chance, and get drowned without her."

I did not trouble myself to make out how much of this was mocking, and as there was no active participation in the joke expected of me, I kept on the safe side of laughing. "No wonder you've been able to do such a lot of pictures," I said. "But I should have thought you might have found it dull--I mean dull together--at odd times."

"Dull?" he shouted. "It's stupendously dull! Especially when our country neighbors come in to "liven us up.' We've got neighbors here that can stay longer in half an hour than most people can in a week. We get tired of each other at times, but after a call from the people in the next house, we return with rapture to our delusion that we are interesting."

"And you never," I ventured, making my jocosity as ironical as possible, "wear upon each other?"

"Horribly!" said Alderling, and his wife smiled contentedly, behind him. "We haven't a whole set of china in the house, from exchanging it across the table, and I haven't made a study of Marion--you must have noticed how many

Marions there were that she hasn't thrown at my head. Especially the Madonnas. She likes to throw the Madonnas at me."

I ventured still farther, addressing myself to Mrs. Alderling. "Does he keep it up all the time--this blague?"

"Pretty much," she answered passively, with entire acquiescence in the fact if it were the fact, or the joke if it were the joke.

"But I didn't see anything of yours, Mrs. Alderling," I said. She had had her talent, as a girl, and some people preferred it to her husband's,--but there was no effect of it anywhere in the house.

"The housekeeping is enough," she answered, with her tranquil smile.

There was nothing in her smile that was leading, and I did not push my inquiry, especially as Alderling did not seem disposed to assist. "Well," I said, "I suppose you will forgive to science my feeling that your situation is most suggestive."

"Oh, don't mind _us!_" said Alderling.

"I won't, thank you," I answered. "Why, it's equal to being cast away together on an uninhabited island."

"Quite," he assented.

"There can't," I went on, "be a corner of your minds that you haven't mutually explored. You must know each other," I cast about for the word, and added abruptly, "by heart."

"I don't suppose he meant anything pretty?" said Alderling, with a look up over his shoulder at his wife; and then he said to me, "We do; and there are some very curious things I could tell you, if Marion would ever let me get in a word."

"Do let him, Mrs. Alderling," I entreated, humoring his joke at her silence.

She smiled, and softly shrugged, and then sighed.

"I could make your flesh creep," he went on, "or I could if you were not a psychologist. I assure you that we are quite weird at times."

"As how?"

"Oh, just knowing what the other is thinking, at a given moment, and saying it. There are times when Marion's thinking is such a nuisance to me, that I have to yell down to her from my loft to stop it. The racket it makes breaks me all up. It's a relief to have her talk, and I try to make her, when she's posing, just to escape the din of her thinking. Then the willing! We experimented with it, after we had first noticed it, but we don't any more. It's too dead easy."

"What do you mean by the willing?" I asked.

"Oh, just wishing one that the other was there, and there he or she is."

"Is he trying to work me, Mrs. Alderling?" I appealed to her, and she answered from her calm:

"It is very unaccountable."

"Then you really mean it! Why can't you give me an illustration?"

"Why, you know," said Alderling more seriously than he had yet spoken, "I don't believe those things, if they are real, can ever be got to show off. That's the reason why your 'Quests in the Occult' are mainly such rubbish, as far as the evidences are concerned. If Marion and I tried to give you an illustration, as you call it, the occult would snub us. But, is there anything so very strange about it? The wonder _is_ that a man and wife ever fail of knowing each what the other is thinking. They pervade each other's minds, if they are really married, and they are so present with each other that the tacit wish should be the same as a call. Marion and I are only an intensified instance of what may be done by living together. There is something, though, that is rather queer, but it belongs to psychomancy rather than psychology, as I understand it."

"Ah!" I said. "What is that queer something?"

"Being visibly present when absent. It has not happened often, but it has happened that I have seen Marion in my loft when she was really somewhere else and not when I had willed her or wished her to be there."

"Now, really," I said, "I must ask you for an instance."

"You want to heap up facts, Lombroso fashion? Well, this is as good as most of Lombroso's facts, or better. I went up one morning, last winter, to work at a study of a Madonna from Marion, directly after breakfast, and left her below in the dining-room, putting away the breakfast things. She has to do that occasionally, between the local helps, who are all we can get in the winter. She professes to like it, but you never can tell, from what a woman says; she has to do it, anyway." It is hard to convey a notion of the serene, impersonal acquiescence of Mrs. Alderling in taking this talk of her. "I was banging away at it when I knew she was behind me looking over my shoulder rather more stormily than she usually does; usually, she is a dead calm. I glanced up, and saw the calm succeed the storm. I kept on, and after awhile I was aware of hearing her step on the stairs."

Alderling stopped, and smoked definitively, as if that were the end.

"Well," I said, after waiting a while, "I don't exactly get the unique value of the incident."

"Oh," he said, as if he had accidentally forgotten the detail, "the steps were coming up?"

"Yes?"

"She opened the door, which she had omitted to do before, and when she came in she denied having been there already. She owned that she had been hurrying through her work, and thinking of mine, so as to make me do something, or undo something, to it; and then all at once she lost her impatience, and came up at her leisure. I don't exactly like to tell what she wanted."

He began to laugh provokingly, and she said, tranquilly, "I don't mind your telling Mr. Wanhope."

"Well, then, strictly in the interest of psychomancy, I will confide that she had found some traces of a model that I used to paint my Madonnas from, before we were married, in that picture. She had slept on her suspicion, and then when she could not stand it any longer, she had come up in the spirit to say that she was not going to be mixed up in a Madonna with any such minx. The words are mine, but the meaning was Marion's. When she found me taking the minx out, she went quietly back to washing her dishes, and then returned in the body to give me a sitting."

III.

We were silent a moment, till I asked, "Is this true, Mrs. Alderling?"

"About," she said. "I don't remember the storm, exactly."

"Well, I don't see why you bother to remain in the body at all," I remarked.

"We haven't arranged just how to leave it together," said Alderling. "Marion, here, if I managed to get off first, would have no means of knowing whether her theory of the effect of my unbelief on my future was right or not; and if _she_ gave _me_ the slip, she would always be sorry that she had not stayed here to convert me."

"Why don't you agree that if either of you lives again, he or she shall make some sign to let the other know?" I suggested. "Well, that has been tried so often, and has it ever worked? It's open to the question whether the dead do not fail to show up because they are forbidden to communicate with the living; and you are just where you were, as to the main point. No, I don't see any way out of it."

Mrs. Alderling went into the house and came out with a book in her hand, and her fingers in it at two places. It was that impressive collection of Christ's words from the New Testament called "The Great Discourse." She put the book before me, first at one place and then at another, and I read, "Whosoever liveth and believeth in me shall never die," and then, "Nay, but except ye repent, ye shall all likewise perish." She did not say anything in showing me these passages, and I found something in her action touchingly childlike and elemental, as well as curiously heathenish. It was as if some poor pagan had brought me his fetish to test its effect upon me. "Yes," I said, "those are things that we hardly know what to do with in our philosophy. They seem to be said as with authority, and yet, somehow, we cannot admit their validity in a philosophical inquiry as to a future life. Aren't they generally taken to mean that we shall be unhappy or happy hereafter, rather than that we shall be or not be at all? And what is believing? Is it the mere act of acknowledgement, or is it something more vital, which expresses itself in conduct?"

She did not try to say. In fact she did not answer at all. Whatever point was in her mind she did not, or could not, debate it. I perceived, in a manner, that her life was so largely subliminal that if she had tried she could not have met my question any more than if she had not had the gift of speech at all. But, in her inarticulate fashion, she had exposed to me a state of mind which I was hardly withheld by the decencies from exploring. "You know," I said, "that psychology almost begins by rejecting the authority of these sayings, and that while we no longer deny anything, we cannot allow anything merely because it has been strongly affirmed. Supposing that there is a life after this, how can it be denied to one and bestowed upon another because one has assented to a certain supernatural claim and another has refused to do so? That does not seem reasonable, it does not seem right. Why should you base your conclusion as to that life upon a promise and a menace which may not really refer to it in the sense which they seem to have?"

"Isn't it all there is?" she asked, and Alderling burst into his laugh.

"I'm afraid she's got you there, Wanhope. When it comes to polemics there's nothing like the passive obstruction of Mrs. Alderling. Marion might never have been an early Christian herself--I think she's an inexpugnable pagan--but she would have gone round making it awfully uncomfortable for the other unbelievers."

"You know," she said to him, and I never could decide how much she was in earnest, "that I can't believe till you do. I couldn't take the risk of keeping on without you."

Alderling followed her in-doors, where she now went to put the book away, with the mock addressed to me, "Did you ever know such a stubborn woman?"

IV.

One conclusion from my observation of the Alderlings during the week I spent with them was that it is bad for a husband and wife to be constantly and unreservedly together, not because they grow tired of each other, but because they grow more intensely interested in each other. Children, when they come, serve the purpose of separating the parents; they seem to unite them in one care, but they divide them in their employments, at least in the normally constituted family. If they are rich, and can throw the care of the children upon servants, then they cannot enjoy the relief from each other that children bring to the mother who nurtures and teaches them, and to the father who must work for them harder than before. The Alderlings were not rich enough to have been freed from the wholesome responsibilities of parentage, but they were childless, and so they were not detached from the perpetual thought of each other. If they had only had different tastes, it might have been better, but they were both artists, she not less than he, though she no longer painted. When their common thoughts were not centred upon each other's being, they were centred on his work, which, viciously enough, was the constant reproduction of her visible personality. I could always see them studying each other, he with an eye to her beauty, she with an eye to his power.

He was every now and then saying to her, "Hold on, Marion," and staying her in some pose or movement, while he made mental note of it, and I was conscious of her preying upon his inmost thoughts and following him into the recesses of his reveries, where it is best for a man to be alone, even if he is sometimes a beast there. She was not like those wives who ask their husbands, when they do not happen to be talking, "What are you thinking about?" and I put this to her credit, till I realized that she had no need to ask, for she knew already. Now and then I saw him get up and shake himself restively, but I am bound to say in her behalf, that her pursuit of him seemed quite involuntary, and that she enjoyed it no more than he did. Twenty times I was on the point of asking, "Why don't you people go in for a good long separation? Is there nothing to call you to Europe, Alderling? Haven't you got a mother, or sister, or some one that you could visit, Mrs. Alderling? It would do you both a world of good."

But it happened, oddly enough, that the Alderlings were as kinless as they were childless, and if he had gone to Europe he would have taken her with him, and prolonged their seclusion by the isolation in which people necessarily live in a foreign country. I found I was the only acquaintance who had visited them during the years of their retirement on the coast, where they had stayed, partly through his inertia, and partly from his superstition that he could paint better away from the ordinary associations and incentives; and they ceased, before I left, to get the good they might of my visit because they made me a part of their intimacy, instead of making themselves part of my strangeness.

After a day or two, their queer experiences began to resume themselves, unabashed by my presence. These were mostly such as they had already more than hinted to me: the thought-transferences, and the unconscious hypnotic suggestions which they made to each other. There was more novelty in the last than the first. If I could trust them, and they did not seem to wish to exploit their mysteries for the effect on me, they were with each other because one or the other had willed it. She would say, if we were sitting together without him, "I think Rupert wants me; I'll be back in a moment," and he, if she were not by, for some time, would get up with, "Excuse me, I must go to Marion; she's calling me."

I had to take a great deal of this on faith; in fact, none of it was susceptible of proof; but I have not been able since to experience all the skepticism which usually replaces the impression left by sympathy with such supposed occurrences. The thing was not quite what we call uncanny; the people were so honest, both of them, that the morbid character of like situations was wanting. The events, if they could be called so, were not invited, I was quite sure, and they were varied by such diversions as we had in reach. I went blueberrying with Mrs. Alderling in the morning after she had got her breakfast dishes put away, in order that we might have something for dessert at our midday dinner; and I went fishing off the old stone crib with Alderling in the afternoon, so that we might have cunners for supper. The farmerfolks and fisherfolks seemed to know them and to be on tolerant terms with them, though it was plain that they still considered them probational in their fellow-citizenship. I do not think they were liked the less because they did not assume to be of the local sort, but let their difference stand, if it would. There was nothing countrified in her dress, which was frankly conventional; the short walking-skirt had as sharp a slant in front as her dinner-gown would have had, and he wore his knickerbockers--it was then the now-faded hour of knickerbockers--with an air of going out golfing in the suburbs. They stood on ceremony in addressing the natives, who might have been Jim or Liza to each other, but were always Mr. Donald or Mrs. Moody, with the Alderlings. They said they would not like being called by their first names themselves, and they did not see why they should take that freedom with others. Neither by nature nor by nurture were they out of the ordinary in their ideals, and it was by a sort of accident that they were so different in their realities. She had stayed on with him through the first winter in the place they had taken for the summer, because she wished to be with him, rather than because she wished to be there, and he had stayed because he had not just found the moment to break away, though afterwards he pretended a reason for staying. They had no more voluntarily cultivated the natural than the supernatural; he kindled the fire for her, and she made the coffee for him, not because they preferred, but because they must; and they had arrived at their common ground in the occult by virtue of being alone together, and not by seeking the solitude for the experiment which the solitude promoted. Mrs. Alderling did not talk less, nor he more, when either was alone with me, than when we were all together; perhaps he was more silent, and she not quite so much; she was making up for him in his absence as he was for her in her presence. But they were always hospitable and attentive hosts, and though under the peculiar circumstances of Mrs. Alderling's having to do the house-work I necessarily had to do a good many things for myself, there were certain little graces which were never wanting, from her hands: my curtains were always carefully drawn, and my coverlet triangularly opened, so that I did not have to pull it down myself. There was a freshly trimmed lamp on the stand at my bed-head, and a book and paper-cutter put there, with a decanter of whiskey and a glass of water. I note these things to you, because they are touches which help remove the sense of anything intentional in the occultism of the Alderlings.

I do not know whether I shall be able to impart the feeling of an obscure pathos in the case of Mrs. Alderling, which I certainly did not experience in Alderling's. Temperamentally he was less fitted to undergo the rigors of their seclusion than she was; in his liking to talk, he needed an audience and a variety of listening, and she, in her somewhat feline calm, could not have been troubled by any such need. You can be silent to yourself, but you cannot very well be loquacious, without danger of having the devil for a listener, if the old saying is true. Yet still, I felt a keener poignancy in her sequestration. Her beauty had even greater claim to regard than his eloquence. She was a woman who could have commanded a whole roomful with it, and no one would have wanted a word from her. She could only have been entirely herself in society, where, and in spite of everything that can be said against it, we can each, if we will, be more natural than out of it. The reason that most of us are not natural in it is that we want to play parts for which we are more or less unfit, and Marion Alderling never wished to play a part, I was sure. It would have sufficed her to be herself wherever she was, and the more people there were by, the more easily she could have been herself.

I am not able to say now how much of all this is observation of previous facts, and how much speculation based upon subsequent occurrences. At the best I can only let it stand for characterization. In the same interest I will add a fact in relation to Mrs. Alderling which ought to have its weight against any undue appeal I have been making in her behalf. Without in the least blaming her, I will say that I think that Mrs. Alderling ate too much. She must have had naturally a strong appetite, which her active life sharpened, and its indulgence formed a sort of refuge from the pressure of the intense solitude in which she lived, and which was all the more a solitude because it was _solitude à deux_. I noticed that beyond the habit of cooks she partook of the dishes she had prepared, and that after Alderling and I had finished dinner, and he was impatient to get at his pipe, she remained prolonging her dessert. One night, when he and I came in from the veranda, she was standing at the sideboard, bent over a saucer of something, and she made me think of a large tortoise-shell cat which has got at the cream. I expected in my nerves to hear her lap, and my expectation was heightened by the soft, purring laugh with which she owned that she was hungry, and those berries were so nice.

At the risk of giving the effect of something sensuous, even sensual, in her, I find myself insisting upon this detail, which did not lessen her peculiar charm. As far as the mystical quality of the situation was concerned, I fancy your finding that rather heightened by her innocent _gourmandise_. You must have noticed how inextricably, for this life at least, the spiritual is trammeled in the material, how personal character and ancestral propensity seem to flow side by side in the same individual without necessarily affecting each other. On the moral side Mrs. Alderling was no more to be censured for the refuge which her nerves sought from the situation in over-eating than Alderling for the smoking in which he escaped from the pressure they both felt from one another; and she was not less fitted than he for their joint experience.

V.

I do not suppose it was with the notion of keeping her weight down that Mrs. Alderling rowed a good deal on the cove before the cottage; but she had a boat, which she managed very well, and which she was out in, pretty much the whole time when she was not cooking, or eating or sleeping, or roaming the berry-pastures with me, or sitting to Alderling for his Madonnas. He did not care for the water himself; he said he knew every inch of that cove, and was tired of it; but he rather liked his wife's going, and they may both have had an unconscious relief from each other in the absences which her excursions promoted. She swam as well as she rowed, and often we saw her going down water-proofed to the shore, where we presently perceived her pulling off in her bathing-dress. Well out in the cove she had the habit of plunging overboard, and after a good swim, she rowed back, and then, discreetly water-proofed again, she climbed the lawn back to the house. Now and then she took me out in her boat, but so far as I remember, Alderling never went with her. Once I ventured to ask him if he never felt anxious about her. He said no, he should not have been afraid to go with her, and she could take better care of herself than he could. Besides, by means of their telepathy they were in constant communion, and he could make her feel at any sort of chance, that he did not wish her to take it, and she would not. This was the only occasion when he treated their peculiar psychomancy boastfully, and the only occasion when I felt a distinct misgiving of his sincerity.

The day before I left, Mrs. Alderling went down about eleven in the morning to her boat, and rowed out into the cove. She rowed far toward the other shore, whither, following her with my eyes from Alderling's window, I saw its ridge blotted out by a long low cloud. It was straight and level as a wall, and looked almost as dense, and I called Alderling.

"Oh, that fog won't come in before afternoon," he said. "We usually get it about four o'clock. But even if it does," he added dreamily, "Marion can manage. I'd trust her anywhere in this cove in any kind of weather."

He went back to his work, and painted away for five or six minutes. Then he asked me, still at the window, "What's that fog doing now?"

"Well, I don't know," I answered. "I should say it was making in."

"Do you see Marion?"

"Yes, she seems to be taking her bath."

Again he painted a while before he asked, "Has she had her dip?"

"She's getting back into her boat."

"All right," said Alderling, in a tone of relief. "She's good to beat any fog in these parts ashore. I wish you would come and look at this a minute."

I went, and we lost ourselves for a time in our criticism of the picture. He was harder on it than I was. He allowed, _"C'est un bon portrait_, as the French used to say of a faithful landscape, though I believe now the portrait can't be too good for them. I can't say about landscape. But in a Madonna I feel that there can be too much Marion, not for me, of course, but for the ideal, which I suppose we are bound to respect. Marion is not spiritual, but I would not have her less of the earth earthy, for all the angels that ever spread themselves 'in strong level flight.'"

I recognized the words from "The Blessed Damozel," and I made bold to be so personal as to say, "If her hair were a little redder than 'the color of ripe corn' one might almost feel that the Blessed Damozel had been painted from Mrs. Alderling. It's the lingering earthiness in her that makes the Damozel so divine."

"Yes, that was a great conception. I wonder none of the fellows do that kind of thing now."

I laughed and said, "Well, so few of them have had the advantage of seeing Mrs. Alderling. And besides, Rosettis don't happen every day."

"It was the period, too. I always tell her that she belongs among the later eighteen sixties. But she insists that she wasn't even born then. Marion is tremendously single-minded."

"She has her mind all on you."

He looked askance at me. "You've noticed--"

"I've noticed that your mind is all on her."

"Not half as much!" he protested, fervidly. "I don't think it's good for her, though of course I like it. That is, in a way. Sometimes it's rather too--" He suddenly flung his brush from him, and started up, with a loudly shouted, "Yes, yes! I'm coming," and hurled himself out of the garret which he used for his studio, and cleared the stairs with two bounds.

By the time I reached the outer door of the cottage, he was a dark blur in the white blur of the fog which had swallowed up the cove, and was rising round the house-walls from the grass. I heard him shouting, "Marion!" and a faint mellow answer, far out in the cove, "Hello!" and then--

"Where are you?" and her answer "Here!" I heard him jump into a boat, and the thump of the oars in the row-locks, and then the rapid beat of the oars while he shouted, "Keep calling!" and she answered,--

"I will!" and called "Hello! Hello! Hello!"

I made my mental comment that this time their mystical means of communication was somehow not working. But after her last hello, no sound broke the white silence of the fog except the throb of Alderling's oars. She was evidently resting on hers, lest she should baffle his attempts to find her by trying to find him.

I suppose ten minutes or so had passed, when the dense air brought me the sound of low laughing that was also like the sound of low sobbing, and then I knew that they had met somewhere in the blind space. I began to hear rowing again, but only as of one boat, and suddenly out of the mist, almost at my feet, Alderling's boat shot up on the shelving beach, and his wife leaped ashore from it, and ran past me up the lawn, while he pulled her boat out on the gravel. She must have been trailing it from the stern of his.

VI.

I was abroad when Mrs. Alderling died, but I heard that it was from a typhoid fever which she had contracted from the water in their well, as was supposed. The water-supply all along that coast is scanty, and that summer most of the wells were dry, and quite a plague of typhoid raged among the people from drinking the dregs. The fever might have gone the worse with her because of her over-fed robustness; at any rate it went badly enough.

I first heard of her death from Minver at the club, and I heard with still greater astonishment that Alderling was down there alone where she had died. Minver said that somebody ought to go down and look after the poor old fellow, but nobody seemed to feel it exactly his office. Certainly I did not feel it mine, and I thought it rather a hardship when a few days after I found a letter from Alderling at the club quite piteously beseeching me to come to him. He had read of my arrival home, in a stray New York paper, and he was firing his letter, he said, at the club, with one chance in a thousand of hitting me with it. Rulledge was by when I read it, and he decided, with that unsparing activity of his, where other people are concerned, that I must go; I certainly could not resist such an appeal as that. He had a vague impression, he said, of something weird in the situation down there, and I ought to go and pull Alderling out of it; besides, I might find my account in it as a psychologist. I hesitated a day, out of self-respect, or self-assertion, and then, the weather coming on suddenly hot, in the beginning of September, I went.

Of course I had meant to go, all along, but I was not so glad when I arrived, as I might have been if Alderling had given me a little warmer welcome. His mood had changed since writing to me, and the strongest feeling he showed at seeing me was what affected me very like a cold surprise.

If I had broken in on a solitude in that place before, I was now the intruder upon a desolation. Alderling was living absolutely alone, except for the occasional presence of a neighboring widow--all the middle-aged women there are widows, with dim or dimmer memories of husbands lost off the Banks, or elsewhere at sea--who came in to get his meals and make his bed, and then had instructions to leave. It was in one of her prevailing absences that I arrived with my bag, and I had to hammer a long time with the knocker on the open door before Alderling came clacking down the stairs in his slippers from the top of the house, and gave me his somewhat defiant greeting. I could almost have said that he did not recognize me at the first bleared glance, and his inability, when he realized who it was, to make me feel at home, encouraged me to take the affair into my own hands.

He looked frightfully altered, but perhaps it was the shaggy beard that he had let grow over his poor, lean muzzle, that mainly made the difference. His clothes hung gauntly upon him, and he had a weak-kneed stoop. His coat sleeves were tattered at the wrists, and one of them showed the white lining at the elbow. I simply shuddered at his shirt.

"Will you smoke?" he asked huskily, almost at the first word, and with an effect of bewilderment in his hospitality that almost made me shed tears.

"Well, not just yet, Alderling," I said. "Shall I go to my old room?"

"Go anywhere," he answered, and he let me carry my bag to the chamber where I had slept before.

It was quite as his wife would have arranged it, even to the detail of a triangular portion of the bedding turned down as she used to do it for me. The place was well aired and dusted, and gave me the sense of being as immaculately clean and fresh as Alderling was not. He sat down in a chair by the window, and he remained, while I laid out my things and made my brief toilet, unabashed by those incidents for which I did not feel it necessary to banish him, if he liked staying.

We had supper by-and-by, a very well-cooked meal of fried fresh cod and potatoes, with those belated blackberries which grow so sweet when they hang long on the canes into September. There was a third plate laid, and I expected that when the housekeeper had put the dishes on the table, she would sit down with us, as the country-fashion still is, but she did not reappear till she came in with the dessert and coffee. Alderling ate hungrily, and much more than I had remembered his doing, but perhaps I formerly had the impression of Mrs. Alderling's fine appetite so strongly in mind that I had failed to note his. Certainly, however, there was a difference in one sort which I could not be mistaken in, and that was in his not talking. Her mantle of silence had fallen upon him, and whereas he used hardly to give me a chance in the conversation, he now let me do all of it. He scarcely answered my questions, and he asked none of his own; but I saw that he liked being talked to, and I did my best, shying off from his sorrow, as people foolishly do, and speaking banalities about my trip to Europe, and the Psychological Congress in Geneva, and the fellows at the club, and heaven knows what rot else.

He listened, but I do not know whether he heard much of my clack, and I got very tired of it myself at last. When I had finished my blackberries, he asked mechanically, in an echo of my former visit, with a repetition of his gesture towards the coffee-pot, "More?" I shook my head, and then he led the way out to the veranda, stopping to get his pipe and tobacco from the mantel on the way. But when we sat down in the early falling September twilight outside, he did not light his pipe, letting me smoke my cigarette alone.

"Are you off your tobacco?" I asked.

"I don't smoke," he answered, but he did not explain why, and I did not feel authorized to ask.

The talk went on as lopsidedly as before, and I began to get sleepy. I made bold to yawn, but Alderling did not mind that, and then I made bold to say that I thought I would go to bed. He followed me indoors, saying that he would go to bed, too. The hall was lighted from a hanging-lamp and two clear-burning hand-lamps which the widow had put for us on a small table. She had evidently gone home, and left us to ourselves. He took one lamp and I the other, and he started up stairs before me. If he were not coming down again, he meant to let the hanging-lamp burn, and I had nothing to say about that; but I suggested, concerning the wide-open door behind me, "Shall I close the door, Alderling?" and he answered, without looking round, "I don't shut it."

He led the way into my room, and he sat down as when I had come, and absently watched my processes of getting into bed. There was something droll, and yet miserable, in his behavior. At first, I thought he might be staying merely for the comfort of a human presence, and again, I thought he might be afraid, for I felt a little creepy myself, for no assignable reason, except that Absence, which he must have been incomparably more sensible of than I. From certain ineffectual movements that he made, and from certain preliminary noises in his throat, which ended in nothing, I decided that he wished to say something to me, tell me something, and could not. But I was selfishly sleepy, and it seemed to me that anything he had on his mind would keep there till morning, at least, and that if he got it off on mine now, it might give me a night of wakeful speculation. So when I got into bed and pulled the sheet up under my chin, I said, "Well, I don't want to turn you out, old fellow."

He stared, and answered, "Oh!" and went without other words, carrying his lamp with him and moving with a weak-kneed shuffle, like a very old man.

He was going to leave the door open behind him, but I called out, "I wish you'd shut me in, Alderling," and after a hesitation, he came back and closed the door.

VII.

We breakfasted as silently on his part as we had supped, but when we had finished, and I was wondering what he was going to let me do with myself, and on the whole what the deuce I had come for, he said, in the longest speech I had yet had from him, "Wouldn't you like to come up and see what I've been doing?"

I said I should like it immensely, and he led the way up stairs, as far As his attic studio. The door of that, like the other doors in the house, stood open, and I got the emotion which the interior gave me, full force, at the first glance. The place was so startlingly alive with that dead woman on a score of canvases in the character in which he had always painted her, that I could scarcely keep from calling out; but I went about, pretending to examine the several Madonnas, and speaking rubbish about them, while he stood stoopingly in the midst of them like the little withered old man he looked. When I had emptied myself of my chaff, I perceived that the time had come.

I glanced about for a seat, and was going to take that in which Mrs. Alderling used to pose for him, but he called out with sudden sharpness, "Not that!" and without appearing to notice, I found a box which I inverted, and sat down on.

"Tell me about your wife, Alderling," I said, and he answered with a sort of scream, "I wanted you to ask me! Why didn't you ask me before? What did you suppose I got you here for?"

With that he shrank down, a miserable heap, in his own chair, and bowed his hapless head and cried. It was more affecting than any notion I can give you of it, and I could only wait patiently for his grief to wash itself out in one of those paroxysms which come to bereavement and leave it somehow a little comforted when they pass.

"I was waiting, for the stupid reasons you will imagine, to let you speak first," I said, "but here in her presence I couldn't hold in any longer."

He asked with strange eagerness, "You noticed that?"

I chose to feign that he meant in the pictures. "Over and over again," I answered.

He would not have my feint. "I don't mean in these wretched caricatures!"

"Well?" I assented provisionally.

"I mean her very self, listening, looking, living--waiting!"

Whether I had insanity or sorrow to deal with, I could not gainsay the unhappy man, and I only said what I really felt: "Yes, the place seems strangely full of her. I wish you would tell me about her."

He asked, with a certain slyness, "Have you heard anything about her already? At the club? From that fool woman in the kitchen?"

"For heaven's sake, no, Alderling!"

"Or about me?"

"Nothing whatever!"

He seemed relieved of whatever suspicion he felt, but he said finally, and with an air of precaution, "I should like to know just how much you mean by the place seeming full of her."

"Oh, I suppose the association of her personality with the whole house, and especially this room. I didn't mean anything preternatural, I believe."

"Then you don't believe in a life after death?" he demanded with a kind of defiance.

I thought this rather droll, seeing what his own position had been, but that was not the moment for the expression of my amusement. "The tendency is to a greater tolerance of the notion," I said. "Men like James and Royce, among the psychologists, and Shaler, among the scientists, scarcely leave us at peace in our doubts, any more, much less our denials."

He said, as if he had forgotten the question: "They called it a very light case, and they thought she was getting well. In fact, she did get well, and then--there was a relapse. They laid it to her eating some fruit which they allowed her."

Alderling spoke with a kind of bitter patience, but in my own mind I was not able to put all the blame on the doctors. Neither did I blame that innocently earthy creature, who was of no more harm in her strong appetite than any other creature which gluts its craving as simply as it feels it. The sense of her presence was deepened by the fact of those childlike self-indulgences which Alderling's words recalled to me. I made no comment, however, and he asked gloomily, as if with a return of his suspicion, "And you haven't heard of anything happening afterward?"

"I don't know what you refer to," I told him, "but I can safely say I haven't, for I haven't heard anything at all."

"They contended that it _didn't_ happen," he resumed. "She died, they said, and by all the tests she had been dead two whole days. She died with her hand in mine. I was not trying to hold her back; she had a kind of majestic preoccupation in her going, so that I would not have dared to detain her if I could. You've seen them go, and how they seem to draw those last, long, deep breaths, as if they had no thought in the world but of the work of getting out of it. When her breathing stopped I expected it to go on, but it did not go on, and that was all. Nothing startling, nothing dramatic, just simple, natural, _like her!_ I gave her hand back, I put it on her breast myself, and crossed the other on it. She looked as if she were sleeping, with that faint color hovering in her face, which was not wasted, but I did not make-believe about it; I accepted the fact of her death. In your 'Quests of the Occult,'" Alderling broke off, with a kind of superiority that was of almost the quality of contempt, "I believe you don't allow yourself to be daunted by a diametrical difference of opinion among the witnesses of an occurrence, as to its nature, or as to its reality, even?" "Not exactly that," I said. "I think I argued that the passive negation of one witness ought not to invalidate the testimony of another as to his experience. One might hear and see things, and strongly affirm them, and another, absorbed in something else, or in a mere suspense of the observant faculties, might quite as honestly declare that so far as his own knowledge was concerned, nothing of the kind happened. I held that in such a case, counter-testimony should not be allowed to invalidate the testimony for the fact."

"Yes, that is what I meant," said Alderling. "You say it more clearly in the book, though."

"Oh, of course."

VIII.

He began again, more remotely from the affair in hand than he had left off, as if he wanted to give himself room for parley with my possible incredulity. "You know how it was with Marion about my not believing that I should live again. Her notion was a sort of joke between us, especially when others were by, but it was a serious thing with her, in her heart. Perhaps it had originally come to her as a mere fancy, and from entertaining it playfully, she found herself with a mental inmate that finally dispossessed her judgment. You remember how literally she brought those Scripture texts to bear on it?"

"Yes. May I say that it was very affecting?"

"Affecting!" Alderling repeated in a tone of amaze at the inadequacy of my epithet. "She was always finding things that bore upon the point. After awhile she got to concealing them, as if she thought they annoyed me. They never did; they amused me; and when I saw that she had something of the sort on her mind, I would say, 'Well, out with it, Marion!' She would always begin, 'Well, you may laugh!'" and as he repeated her words Alderling did laugh, forlornly, and as I must say, rather bloodcurdlingly.

I could not prompt him to go on, but he presently did so himself, desolately enough. "I suppose, if I was in her mind at all in that supreme moment, when she seemed to be leaving this life behind with such a solemn effect of rating it at nothing, it may have been a pang to her that I was not following her into the dark, with any ray of hope for either of us. She could not have returned from it with the expectation of convincing me, for I used to tell her that if one came back from the dead, I should merely know that he had been mistaken about being dead, and was giving me a dream from his trance. She once asked me if I thought Lazarus was not really dead, with a curious childlike interest in the miracle, and she was disheartened when I reminded her that Lazarus had not testified of any life hereafter, and it did not matter whether he had been really dead or not when he was resuscitated, as far as that was concerned. Last year, we read the Bible a good deal together here, and to tease her I pretended to be convinced of the contrary by the very passages that persuaded her. As she told you, she did not care for herself. You remember that?"

"Distinctly," I said.

"It was always so. She never cared. I was perfectly aware that if she could have assured life hereafter to me, she would have given her life here to do it. You know how some women, when they are married, absolutely give themselves up, try to lose themselves in the behoof of their husbands? I don't say it rightly; there are no words that will express the utterness of their abdication."

"I know what you mean," I said, "and it was one of the facts which most interested me in Mrs. Alderling."

"Because I wasn't worthy of it? No man is!"

"It wasn't a question of that in my mind; I don't believe that occurred to me. It was the _Ding an sich_ that interested me, or as it related itself to her, and not the least as it related itself to you. Such a woman's being is a cycle of self-sacrifice, so perfect, so essential, from birth to death, as to exclude the notion of volition. She is what she does. Of course she has to put her sacrifice into words from time to time, but its true language is acts, and the acts themselves only clumsily express it. There is a kind of tyranny in it for the man, of course. It requires self-sacrifice to be sacrificed to, and I don't suppose a woman has any particular merit in what is so purely natural. It appears pathetic when it is met with ingratitude or rejection, but when it has its way it is no more deserving our reverence than eating or sleeping. It astonishes men because they are as naturally incapable of it as women are capable of it." I was mounted and was riding on, forgetful of Alderling, and what he had to tell me, if he had anything, but he recalled me to myself by having apparently forgotten me, for when I paused, he took up his affair at a quite different point, and as though that were the question in hand.

"That gift, or knack, or trick, or whatever it was, of one compelling the presence of the other by thinking or willing it, was as much mine as hers, and she tried sometimes to get me to say that I would use it with her if she died before I did; and if she were where the conditions were opposed to her coming to me, my will would help her to overcome the hinderance; our united wills would form a current of volition that she could travel back on against all obstacles. I don't know whether I make myself clear?" he appealed.

"Yes, perfectly," I said. "It is very curious." He said in a kind of muse, "I don't know just where I was." Then he began again, "Oh, yes! It was at the ceremony--down there in the library. Some of the country people came in; I suppose they thought they ought, and I suppose they wanted to; it didn't matter to me. I had sent for Doctor Norrey, as soon as the relapse came, and he was there with me. Of course there was the minister, conducting the services. He made a prayer full of helpless repetitions, which I helplessly noticed, and some scrambling remarks, mostly misdirected at me, affirming and reaffirming that the sister they had lost was only gone before, and that she was now in a happier world.

"The singing and the praying and the preaching came to an end, and then there was that soul-sickening hush, that exanimate silence, of which the noise of rustling clothes and scraping feet formed a part, as the people rose in the hall, where chairs had been put for them, leaving me and Norrey alone with Marion. Every fibre of my frame recognized the moment of parting, and protested. A tremendous wave of will swept through me and from me, a resistless demand for her presence, and it had power upon her. I heard her speak, and say, as distinctly as I repeat the words, 'I will come for you!' and the youth and the beauty that had been growing more and more wonderful in her face, ever since she died, shone like a kind of light from it. I answered her, 'I am ready now!' and then Norrey scuffled to his feet, with a conventional face of sympathy, and said, 'No hurry, my dear Alderling,' and I knew he had not heard or seen anything, as well as I did afterwards when I questioned him. He thought I was giving them notice that they could take her away. What do you think?"

"How what do I think?" I asked.

"Do you think that it happened?"

There was something in Alderling's tone and manner that made me, instead of answering directly that I did not, temporize and ask, "Why?"

"Because--because," and Alderling caught his breath, like a child that is trying to keep itself from crying, "because _I_ don't." He broke into a sobbing that seemed to wrench and tear his poor little body, and if I had thought of anything to say, I could not have said it to his headlong grief with any hope of assuaging it. "I am satisfied now," he said, at last, wiping his wet face, and striving for some composure of its trembling features, "that it was all a delusion, the effect of my exaltation, of my momentary aberration, perhaps. Don't be afraid of saying what you really think," he added scornfully, "with the notion of sparing me. You couldn't doubt it, or deny it, more completely than I do."

I confess this unexpected turn struck me dumb. I did not try to say anything, and Alderling went on.

"I don't deny that she is living, but I can't believe that I shall ever live to see her again, or if you prefer, die to see her. There is the play of the poor animal instinct, or the mechanical persistence of expectation in me, so that I can't shut the doors without the sense of shutting her out, can't put out the lights without feeling that I am leaving her in the dark. But I know it is all foolishness, as well as you do, all craziness. If she is alive it is because she believed she should live, and I shall perish because I didn't believe. I should like to believe, now, if only to see her again, but it is too late. If you disuse any member of your body, or any faculty of your mind, it withers away and if you deny your soul your soul ceases to be."

I found myself saying, "That is very interesting," from a certain force of habit, which you have noted in me, when confronted with a novel instance of any kind. "But," I suggested, "why not act upon the reverse of that principle, and create the fact by affirmation which you think your denial destroys?"

"Because," he repeated wearily, "it is too late. You might as well ask the fakir who has held his arm upright for twenty years, till it has stiffened there, to restore the dry stock by exercise. It is too late, I tell you."

"But, look here, Alderling," I pursued, beginning to taste the joy of argument. "You say that your will had such power upon her after you knew her to be dead that you made her speak to you?"

"No, I don't say that now," he returned. "I know now that it was a delusion."

"But if you once had that power of summoning her to you, by strongly wishing for her presence, when you were both living here, why doesn't it stand to reason that you could do it still, if she is living there and you are living here?"

"I never had any such power," he replied, with the calm of absolute tragedy. "That was a delusion too. I leave the doors open for her, night and day, because I must, but if she came I should know it was not she."

IX.

Of course you know your own business, my dear Acton, but if you think of using the story of the Alderlings--and there is no reason why you should not, for they are both dead, without kith or kin surviving, so far as I know, unless he has some relatives in Germany, who would never penetrate the disguise you could give the case--it seems to me that here is your true climax. But I necessarily leave the matter to you, for I shall not touch it at any point where we could come into competition. In fact, I doubt if I ever touch it at all, for though all psychology is in a manner dealing with the occult, still I think I have done my duty by that side of it, as the occult is usually understood; and I am shy of its grosser instances, as things that are apt to bring one's scientific poise into question. However, you shall be the judge of what is best for you to do, when you have the whole story, and I will give it you without more ado, merely premising that I have a sort of shame for the aptness of the catastrophe. I shall respect you more if I hear that you agree with me as to the true climax of the tragedy, and have the heroism to reject the final event.

I stayed with Alderling nearly a week, and I will own that I bored myself. In fact, I am not sure but we bored each other. At any rate, when I told him, the night before I intended going, that I meant to leave him in the morning, he seemed resigned, or indifferent, or perhaps merely inattentive. From time to time we had recurred to the matter of his experience, or his delusion, but with apparently increasing impatience on his part, and certainly decreasing interest on mine; so that at last I think he was willing to have me go. But in the morning he seemed reluctant, and pleaded with me to stay a few days longer with him. I alleged engagements, more or less unreal, for I was never on such terms with Alderling that I felt I need make any special sacrifice to him. He gave way, suspiciously, rather, and when I came down from my room after having put the last touches to my packing, I found him on the veranda looking out to seaward, where a heavy fog-bank hung.

You will sense here the sort of _patness_ which I feel cheapens the catastrophe; and yet, as I consider it, again, the fact is not without its curious importance, and its bearing upon what went before. I do not know but it gives the whole affair a relief which it would not otherwise have.

He was to have driven me to the station, some miles away, before noon, and I supposed we should sit down together, and try to have some sort of talk before I went. But Alderling appeared to have forgotten about my going, and after a while, took himself off to his studio, and left me alone to watch the inroads of the fog. It came on over the harbor rapidly, as on that morning when Mrs. Alderling had been so nearly lost in it, and presently the masts and shrouds of the shipping at anchor were sticking up out of it as if they were sunk into a body as dense as the sea under them.

I amused myself watching it blot out one detail of the prospect after another, while the fog-horn lowed through it, and the bell-buoy, far out beyond the light-house ledge, tolled mournfully. The milk-white mass moved landward, and soon the air was blind with the mist which hid the grass twenty yards away. There was an awfulness in the silence, which nothing broke but the lowing of the horn, and the tolling of the bell, except when now and then the voice of a sailor came through it, like that of some drowned man sending up his hail from the bottom of the bay.

Suddenly I heard a joyful shout from the attic overhead:

"I am coming! I am coming!"

It was Alderling calling out through his window, and then a cry came from over the water, which seemed to answer him, but which there is no reason in the world to believe was not a girlish shout from one of the yachts, swallowed up in the fog.

His lunging descent of the successive stairways followed, and he burst through the doorway beside me, and without heeding me, ran bareheaded down the sloping lawn.

I followed, with what notion of help or hinderance I should not find it easy to say, but before I reached the water's edge--in fact I never did reach it, and had some difficulty making my way back to the house,--I heard the rapid throb of the oars in the row-locks as he pulled through the white opacity.

You know the rest, for it was the common property of our enterprising press at the time, when the incident was fully reported, with my ineffectual efforts to be satisfactorily interviewed as to the nothing I knew.

The oarless boat was found floating far out to sea after the fog lifted. It was useless to look for Alderling's body, and I do not know that any search was made for it.

9 781835 915066